jimmy fox and the flying falcon

jimmy fox and the flying falcon

By Don Dwiggins

Illustrated by Olga Dwiggins

A Golden Gate Junior Book
Childrens Press Chicago

Library of Congress Cataloging in Publication Data

Dwiggins, Don.
Jimmy Fox and the Flying Falcon.

"A Golden Gate junior book."
SUMMARY: Although Jimmy has had instruction, his first solo sailplane flight on his fourteenth birthday is almost more than he can deal with.
[1. Gliding—Fiction] I. Dwiggins, Olga. II. Title.
PZ7.D9597Ji [Fic] 77-24301
ISBN 0-516-08826-2

Published simultaneously in Canada
Printed in the United States of America
Designed by Jon Ritchie

To Patrick

contents

jimmy fox and the flying falcon

the big air race

Jimmy Fox leaned against the big hangar door. He made his hands into tight fists. He held his breath. He knew exactly what was going to happen next. He counted slowly, "One . . . two . . . three . . . four"

Jimmy stared up at the sky. The tiny red biplane was coming down, down, down, with black smoke behind it. It spun around and around, growing larger and larger.

Hundreds of pairs of eyes looked up. A hush fell over the people in the grandstand. A dozen rows of wooden seats in front of the hangar were filled with visitors to the airfield. Jimmy knew that many of them came to see blood.

"Oh, please! Don't crash!" he cried to himself. He could see Bud Horner in the cockpit. His head was bent forward as he looked out of the airplane.

It was the thrilling climax to Bud's Air Show. Each time, it seemed to Jimmy, Bud came closer to death. Each time he pulled out closer to the ground. Would he make it this time?

Jimmy shut his eyes. He didn't want to watch. But he could not shut out the voice of his father, Frank Fox. It boomed through the loudspeaker. "Watch him cheat death!" the voiced cried. "Watch Bud Horner's famous Spin of Death! *Will he make it?"*

Jimmy heard the crowd gasp. The little biplane seemed to spin even faster. He opened his eyes now, watching in terror. "Pull out! Pull out!" he shouted, even though he knew Bud couldn't hear him.

At the last second the little airplane stopped spinning. It came low across the runway, still with black smoke behind it. Then it went up again.

"Let's give Bud Horner a big hand," Frank Fox yelled through the loudspeaker. "No other living pilot can do the Spin of Death the way he can!"

The people watching stood up and cheered. Jimmy felt proud. He liked Bud. The young pilot was almost part of the Fox family.

"And now, ladies and gentlemen," his father's voice went on, "you'll see Deborah Fox. She is Queen of the Air. She will ride through a loop—standing on the top of the wing *without a parachute!*"

"On, no!" Jimmy cried to himself. "Please, Dad, don't let Mom do this one without a chute!"

He watched Frank Fox climb into the cockpit of the big Stearman biplane. Tears came to his eyes. He could hardly see his mother as she took her place on the top wing.

Jimmy's sister Frances was at the microphone now. She was telling the

crowd what would happen next. Frances was sixteen years old and already a good pilot. She'd learned from Bud Horner. He taught people to fly at the little airport in the California desert. It was called Morning Sun Airfield. It was the same airfield where Jimmy's father had taught Air Cadets to fly during World War II. He had bought it after the war ended.

Jimmy believed his father was the greatest pilot in the world. But why, today, was he taking such chances? Jimmy turned and ran. He did not want to see this next event. It always made his blood chill and left an ache in his stomach.

He knew that the Morning Sun Air Show drew lots of people to the little airfield. Some of them would come back later to learn to fly. That was what the Air Show was for.

Jimmy hated it. But he liked the way the Flying Foxes could fly airplanes. That's what they were called on the big posters that told about the Air Show. Jimmy was the youngest of the family. They couldn't really be *The Flying Foxes* without him!

Jimmy ran as fast as he could, out

across the desert. He threw himself down on the ground. He stared up at the sky. At thirteen he was no longer a child. But being a teen-ager was a whole new thing. Sometimes Jimmy felt he was nothing at all. He knew he couldn't even fly a glider by himself until he was fourteen. And he'd have to be at least sixteen before he could fly an airplane with an engine in it. Oh sure, his father took him up for rides lots of times. Sometimes he even let him fly the plane. But what Jimmy wanted most in the world was to *really* learn to fly.

Sometimes he felt like a stranger. Only last week he'd gone into the hangar to ask his dad when he could start taking flying lessons. There was a big canvas curtain hanging down from the ceiling. When he'd asked what was behind the curtain his father had said, "This is off limits, Jimmy. You're not supposed to be back here!"

Now, in the distance, he could hear his sister's voice on the loudspeaker. "Keep your eyes on the Stearman," she cried. "Watch closely! There's Debbie Fox, standing on the top wing! Without a parachute!"

In spite of himself, Jimmy's eyes were drawn to that part of the sky where the roaring Stearman was suddenly diving. It had smoke coming from it. He could see the tiny figure in white on the top wing. He sat up. This time he couldn't look away. The Stearman climbed straight up. Then it went over on its back, upside down. "Dad!" Jimmy cried aloud. "She's not wearing her chute!"

The pencil line of smoke went over and down. It traced a perfect circle in the sky. Jimmy knew that his mother would not fall off. That is, if everything went right! Something his dad called centrifugal force would hold her to the wing.

Jimmy turned his back. He remembered something else his father had told him. ‘‘All these stunts really aren’t stunts, Jimmy. A stunt pilot is just a showoff. A crazy fool trying to draw attention to himself. An airplane flies according to fixed rules,’’ he had said. ‘‘A good pilot must know those rules by heart. When he goes against the rules he’s in bad trouble.’’

Jimmy heard the roar of the crowd as his father landed the Stearman. Nothing had gone wrong. He knew his mother would be smiling and waving, just as she always did. He put his hands over his ears. He didn’t want to hear any more. Some of the crowd were yelling for blood. They had come to see an accident, Jimmy felt sure.

The next big event was the thing Jimmy feared the most. The midget plane race. Six tiny planes would fly over the desert only a few feet above the ground.

They would fly in a tight circle around four pylons. The pylons were small wooden towers covered with canvas. They were painted with red and white checkers so the pilots could see them easily. At 200 miles an hour the flyers had to see the pylons very quickly.

Jimmy always thrilled to see the tiny racers speeding around the pylons. He looked away from the airfield. To his left, a pylon stuck up into the sky. Its red and white paint made a wild pattern in the sun.

The pylon was called the scatter pylon. It was the first one the racers would head for. All of them would take off together in what Jimmy's father called a race horse start. They would try to be first around the scatter pylon. Then they'd come speeding back to cross the starting line.

It was almost race time. Jimmy forgot everything else now. He could see the

tiny airplanes in the distance. They were lined up side by side in front of the grandstand. He checked his watch. The hands told him it was almost 10 o'clock. When the big second hand went around once more it would be exactly race time.

He heard the starter gun. Then the roar of six engines rolled across the desert. Jimmy saw the planes coming. They came straight towards him. They were so low he could read the names on their sides.

In the lead was a shiny plane. Its wings looked like two silver swords. Number 13 was Bud Horner's racer. It was named *Frances* for Jimmy's sister.

Behind it came a racer painted black. It was Wilson Gorman's. Gorman was a hard-flying pilot who ran another airport not far from the Morning Sun. Jimmy didn't like him. Once he had bawled out Jimmy and a friend when they'd crossed his field during a hike. But, most of all,

Jimmy was sure he didn't play fair. He knew that both his dad and Gorman wanted the same small airmail route up the valley. But, unlike Frank Fox, Gorman would stop at nothing to get his way. And he'd probably get it, too, Jimmy thought bitterly.

Behind Bud and Gorman came the others. Some were famous pilots whose names Jimmy knew by heart. The racers swept around behind the scatter pylon. Then they headed towards the starting line. Bud Horner was holding his lead. Gorman was close on his tail. The others were coming up fast.

It would be a ten-lap race. Each plane would have to fly around all four pylons ten times. Then they would finish in front of the grandstand. The course was half a mile long. The planes would cover a full mile in going around the pylons.

Jimmy watched them coming down the back stretch. Bud Horner and Wilson

Gorman were flying wingtip to wingtip. Bud was on the inside. The two men were pulling away from the others.

The far pylon at the end of the back stretch was a dangerous corner, Jimmy saw. The planes would be turning across the wind. If the pilots cut too close to the pylon they could crash into it. "Look out, Bud!" Jimmy yelled. He had seen Number 10 bank suddenly. It turned toward Bud's racer, forcing it too close to the pylon.

It seemed certain that Bud would crash into the pylon. At the last second he went low. His left wingtip almost hit the desert floor as Gorman's black plane flew past him.

Gorman had the lead now. The two racers were battling for first place. They came around the third pylon, turning back toward the airport. Gorman held his lead. Number 13 was close behind. One by one the others roared around the third pylon.

Jimmy held his breath as the ships circled the far pylons once more. Jimmy saw that Bud had dropped back. His ship was going higher.

On the next lap Jimmy saw what Bud was up to. His plane dove toward the third pylon — just as Gorman's black racer flew around it like an ugly sword. Bud came even closer to the pylon. He cut inside Gorman's plane, going past with extra speed from the dive. Number 13 was winning!

Now the other racers were gaining on Gorman. But Number 13 was well out in front. It went for the home stretch. If Bud could hold his lead he'd win the race and the prize money.

Then Jimmy cried out. Black smoke came from Gorman's plane. His engine was on fire! He saw Gorman pull out of the race. He was going to try to land in a nearby field. The black plane hit the ground. It bounced high into the air.

Then it tumbled end over end and came to rest upside down.

Bud's plane was still well ahead, but it now left the race. It flew toward the black smoke from the wreck. "Bud!" Jimmy cried. "Don't quit the race! You're winning!"

Jimmy ran as hard as he could. He ran across the rocky field toward Gorman's black plane. He saw Number 13 above him. Bud was going to land in the softer sand close by.

Jimmy could see Gorman through the plane's plexiglass canopy. The man was trying to get out. But the plane was upside down. Gorman was trapped. Smoke and flames started quickly. Jimmy thought fast. Soon the flames would reach the gas tank. Then the whole ship would explode. *He had to get Gorman out*.

He picked up a heavy rock. He ran with it, straight into the thick smoke. He

could feel the heat, but he kept right on. He stopped close by the wreck. He threw the rock as hard as he could against the plane's canopy. It broke open. Gorman fell out onto the ground.

Jimmy grabbed Gorman's arm. He

tried to pull him away from the flames but the man was too heavy. Then he heard Bud's voice. "Get back, Jimmy!"

Bud was running toward him at top speed. Jimmy began to cough. The smoke was filling his lungs. But he still tugged at Gorman's arm. Bud was there now. He grabbed Gorman's other arm. Together they pulled him away. By now he had fainted.

Bud laid Gorman on the ground behind a big rock. A second later the plane blew up.

Gorman opened his eyes. He looked up at Jimmy and Bud. "Thanks," he said.

Jimmy felt proud of Bud. "You lost the race, Bud. You could have won," he said.

Bud laughed. "Winning isn't everything, Jimmy."

They heard the ambulance coming. Gorman would be all right. His left leg was broken. He wouldn't be flying for a few months. But they had saved his life — and that was what mattered.

jimmy meets the flying falcon

"You were a real hero, Jimmy," Frances Fox smiled across the table at her brother. It was the evening after the air show. The Fox family had gathered for a big dinner in Jimmy's honor.

"Thanks, Sis," Jimmy said. "But it really wasn't all that much. Bud did the big thing. He carried Mr. Gorman away from the plane in time."

"Mr. Gorman owes his life to you two," his mother said. "Both you and Bud should be proud."

Jimmy shook his head. "I guess not. He'll just make more trouble — like today."

"Jimmy! That's no way to talk." Frank Fox's voice was harsh.

"But he was risking Bud's life, trying to win the race," Jimmy said loudly. "What happened served him right!"

"Son, I know the accident was a terrible shock to you," his mother said. "Sometimes after a shock we say things we don't mean."

"But I *do* mean it!" Jimmy said. "Sure, I'm glad I helped save him. But he'll just be mad he lost the race."

"Now Jimmy," his mother went on. "Mr. Gorman knows he only had bad luck."

"Yes! And he'll bring *us* bad luck, too!" Jimmy almost shouted. He pushed away from the table and got up to leave.

"You're not excused, Jimmy," his father said. "Sit down." Jimmy sat down, his eyes on his plate. Why were they making such a fuss over him?

"I have something to show you, son,"

his father went on. "I've been keeping it as a surprise. But I think now's the time to show it to you. Tell your mother you're sorry for the way you talked. Then come with me."

Jimmy followed his father outside the small white house that was their home at Morning Sun Airfield. The two walked together toward the big hangar. Jimmy's heart beat a little faster. Surely now he was going to know what was behind that curtain inside the hangar!

"Come sit down over here, Jimmy," his father said as he closed the hangar door. "We have a few things to talk about before you see the surprise."

"If it's about Mr. Gorman, Dad, I've had my say," Jimmy began.

Frank Fox shook his head. "That's settled, I think," he said. "I know that you were worried about Bud today. But he can take care of himself. It's you I'm thinking of."

Jimmy sat down next to his father. He wondered what was on his father's mind. It sounded serious. "Son," his father went on to say, "it may be that you're growing up too fast. Life around an airport may be too hard on you."

"No, Dad!" Jimmy said. "I love it here! And now that school's out I can spend all summer helping you and Bud. I want to know *everything* about airplanes—"

"I know you do. And I think you've got what it takes to be a good pilot someday," Frank Fox said. "But you've got to learn to hold your temper. There's no place in the sky for anger. You've got to learn to keep a cool head."

Jimmy kicked at a piece of wood on the floor. He sent it skipping toward the big canvas curtain. "I'll really try, Dad," he said.

"Look here, Jimmy," Frank Fox went on. "I'm going to bring this up once more after all. Then we'll drop it for good. Wilson Gorman means well, but he tries too hard. You can't make things happen by pushing people around. If you do, sooner or later you're in trouble.''

''You mean like forcing Bud into the pylon today?'' Jimmy asked.

''Well, yes. That and more. Wilson Gorman and I are trying to win the same government airmail contract. There isn't room for two planes on that short run.''

''Mr. Gorman will be in the hospital for quite awhile, Dad,'' Jimmy said. ''Maybe we can win the contract ahead of him.''

His father shook his head. ''You know that wouldn't be fair, Jimmy. We'll just have to wait until he gets well. Then we'll see who can make the best offer.''

Jimmy was quiet. He and his father had not often talked about grown-up things like this. He felt proud. His father was sharing his real thoughts with him.

''But to get back to you, Jimmy,''

Frank went on. "You're almost fourteen, aren't you?"

"I'll be fourteen in September," Jimmy answered. "September the fifteenth."

"You know you can't fly a plane by yourself until you're fourteen, don't you?"

"Sure, I know that. And then I can only do it in an old glider," Jimmy answered.

"And what's wrong with a glider?" Frank Fox was smiling now.

"It doesn't even have an engine!" Jimmy cried. "A glider's not a real airplane at all."

His father laughed. "Well, son, perhaps you don't know that some of the greatest pilots who ever lived have flown gliders. Gliders that can ride the winds for hours are called sailplanes. For example, Charles Lindbergh happened to be an expert sailplane pilot. And the

Wright brothers were flying gliders long before they put an engine in their plane down at Kitty Hawk.''

''I knew that, Dad. But you can't *go* anywhere in a sailplane until the winds are right.''

''That's the whole idea,'' his father said. ''A sailplane pilot is the true master of the sky. Like an eagle. He doesn't *need* an engine. He can look up at the sky and see things other pilots don't even know about.''

''Like what?'' Jimmy asked.

''Well, a sailplane pilot studies the clouds. If they pile up high, like a dish of ice cream, he knows there's warm air pushing up under them. He calls the bubble of air a thermal. He can slide his plane over into the thermal and circle way up into the sky — like eagles do.''

Frank Fox stood up. ''But that's enough talk for now, Jimmy,'' he said.

“It’s time you saw what it is I brought you out here for.”

Jimmy followed his father to the back of the hangar where the canvas curtain hung. Frank pulled it back.

"Dad!" Jimmy cried. He ran forward. Then he stopped, his mouth wide open. A sleek sailplane sat there. Its long, slender wings stretched from one side of the hangar to the other. Jimmy circled it slowly. He studied its graceful lines. It was painted white. It reminded him of a sea gull.

"Dad, it's beautiful," he said at last, almost in a whisper.

His father placed a hand on his shoulder. "It's yours, Jimmy. All yours."

"Thank you," Jimmy said. He couldn't think of anything else to say.

He walked around the sailplane again. He tapped the wing. He looked into the cockpit. It had two seats, one in front of the other. He looked underneath, at the single landing wheel.

"The reason Bud and I kept this a secret from you, son," his father said as he watched Jimmy, "was because we wanted you to have it when it was all ready to fly. It took quite a while to build and paint. But it's ready and waiting for you now. There's only one more thing to do. That's to name the plane. What are you going to call it?''

Jimmy thought a moment. Suddenly he remembered a graceful falcon he'd seen flying across the desert. ''I'd like to call it the *Flying Falcon,* Dad,'' he said.

His father nodded. Then he went over to the work bench in the corner. He came back with a can of red paint and a brush. Carefully he painted the name on each side of the glider's nose — FLYING FALCON.

''Dad, when can we fly it?'' Jimmy asked eagerly.

''It's too late this evening, of course,'' Frank answered. ''We'll take her up tomorrow, bright and early. That is, if you want to.''

''If I *want* to?'' Jimmy shouted. ''Dad, I can hardly wait!''

The sun had set behind the mountain when Jimmy came to a big joshua tree out by the plane wreck. He sat down on a rock near it. He wanted to think about all that had happened that day. He looked up at the sky. Then he noticed a nest of sticks and leaves up near the top of the joshua tree. A falcon's nest!

The golden light in the sky made the joshua look as if it were on fire. The mother falcon was nowhere to be seen. Jimmy wondered about the little falcon chicks in the nest. He could see three tiny heads poking up, three hungry beaks wide open.

Then he heard a sound close by. A tiny cry. He looked around. But he could see nothing. The cry came again. Jimmy turned his head. He got up and tiptoed to the brush at the base of the joshua.

Caught in a tangle of thorny branches was a tiny bird. A baby falcon! Its pin feathers barely covered its pink skin. Its

little beak opened wide. An angry cry came from its throat. Jimmy picked up the little bird. He cupped it in his hands. It kicked and struggled. "Pipe down, little feller," Jimmy said softly. "I won't hurt you."

Jimmy looked up at the sky. The mother falcon was nowhere in sight. The joshua was too tall, too thorny for Jimmy to climb, holding the baby bird. He couldn't put it back in the nest. And of course it would be dangerous to leave it in the brush. The night animals would soon be out hunting.

Jimmy turned and ran toward the big hangar. Carefully, he held the baby bird inside his shirt. The bird squirmed and scratched. Jimmy didn't mind. He knew what he wanted to do. He'd take care of the fuzzy little bird himself. He'd raise it to become big and strong.

That night Jimmy lay in bed, still thinking of his exciting day. He thought about the beautiful new glider — the *Flying Falcon*. Soon he'd *really* be one of the Flying Foxes. And then there was the baby falcon to take care of — and maybe teach to fly!

jimmy learns to fly

Jimmy Fox was out in the big hangar long before the sun came up. Night chill still hung in the air. In the back of the hangar the *Flying Falcon* looked like a gray ghost in the dim light.

Jimmy moved to the big cardboard box in the corner. He looked inside, through the chicken wire. The baby bird was safe. He opened the box and picked up the little falcon. "You and I are going to learn to fly together," he said softly. "Think of the fun we'll have!'

The bird needs a name, Jimmy thought. Sam was a good name. He'd call him Sam. He put the falcon back in his box.

He turned to the sailplane and opened the canopy.

Jimmy climbed into the front seat. It was just the right size with a cushion behind him. He stretched out his legs. His feet rested on the rudder pedals.

"Morning, Jimmy!"

Jimmy looked up and smiled. His father came toward him, through the big hangar doors.

"Morning, Dad! I was just looking over the *Flying Falcon!*"

"That's the way, Jimmy," his father said. "A good pilot takes time to learn where everything is in the cockpit. Then he can fly almost by instinct."

"You mean—like a bird? Like Sam?"

Frank Fox laughed. "I see you've got a new friend."

"We're going to learn to fly together," Jimmy said.

"That's fine. But I'll bet that bird teaches you more than you can teach him!"

Jimmy frowned. "Maybe, Dad. If Sam's wings were full grown, he wouldn't have fallen out of his nest. Anyway, he could have flown right back up!"

"Sam's wings are special," his father said. "They're long and narrow, for soaring. Just like the wing on your sailplane. But come on, Jimmy. The sun's up. It's time to find out how the *Flying Falcon* really flies!"

They rolled open the hangar doors and pushed the *Flying Falcon* outside. Jimmy's father went back to the house. Bud Horner was just finishing breakfast. "Got a job for you, Bud," Frank said. "You're to fly the towplane today. Jimmy and I are taking up the sailplane."

Bud stood up. "Great! I'll bet Jimmy's excited!"

The sun was climbing high by the time they were set to go. The *Flying Falcon* stood at the end of the runway. The Piper Super Cub towplane was parked in front of it. The two aircraft were linked by a rope.

Jimmy took his place in the front seat. He carefully hooked his seat belt. His back-pack parachute felt good. Frank Fox climbed in back. He strapped himself down, then wiggled the rear control stick.

"All set, Jimmy?"

"All set, Dad!"

Jimmy watched the Super Cub begin to move ahead slowly, taking up slack in the tow rope.

"Keep the wings level, Jimmy!" his father called.

Jimmy held the stick with care. He felt it come to life as the *Flying Falcon* picked up speed. Quickly the sailplane lifted from the runway. Then Jimmy saw the towplane leave the ground. He steered the sailplane right behind it.

"Just keep your wings even with Bud's," Frank Fox said. "If he banks to the left, you bank too, just the same amount!"

Jimmy's heart beat fast. Higher and higher they climbed above the airfield. The towplane led them off toward West

Mountain, bright in the morning sun. They were flying 2,000 feet above the desert floor now.

"You've got to remember several things at once when you're flying," his father told Jimmy. "Your air speed. Your compass heading. The way you're headed. The sailplane's attitude."

Jimmy already knew about attitude, from flying in his father's Stearman. Attitude meant keeping the nose right on the horizon, the wings level. If the nose got too high, the ship would slow down — and maybe stall. Just like a car trying to go up a hill that was too steep.

"It's time to cut loose, Jimmy," his father said. "Pull the red handle on your left. That will set you free. Then bank away to the right."

The tow rope let go with a loud bang. Jimmy pulled back on the stick and put the *Flying Falcon* into a climbing turn to the right.

Soon the sailplane settled down into a glide. Its air speed was 80 miles an hour. Jimmy loved the soft whisper of the wind. He swept the *Flying Falcon* around in easy turns as they glided lower and lower.

"Tomorrow afternoon we'll go up and look for some thermals, Jimmy," his father said. "Remember what I've told you? Thermals are rising bubbles of warm air, the kind hawks soar in. But let's head back and land now. We're getting too low."

Frank Fox took the controls. He showed Jimmy how to enter the airport traffic pattern, how to dive a little for extra speed. "When you're sure you can make the field, Jimmy, open the spoilers. They stick up along the top of the wing — and they let you sink faster. Your extra air speed gives you extra safety."

This was not like flying a powered plane, Jimmy saw. Instead of slowing

FLYING FALCON

down in the traffic pattern, you speeded up in a sailplane.

He saw the runway ahead of them. Part way down the runway, he could see two white lines. "Let's see if we can land right between those lines, Jimmy," his father said.

Frank Fox helped Jimmy guide the sailplane toward the white lines. He used the spoilers just enough to let the plane settle onto the runway. As the landing wheel touched the ground, Jimmy felt his father push forward on the stick. The *Flying Falcon* rose up onto its hickory nose skid. It rolled up onto the parking ramp and came to a stop directly in front of the hangar.

"You'll learn fast, Jimmy," his father said, after they'd tied down the *Flying Falcon*.

Walking back to the house, Jimmy asked, "Dad, can I take Sam up for a ride next time?"

Frank Fox laughed. ''I think you'd better wait awhile, Jimmy, at least until his wing feathers are grown. You've only begun to learn about flying. You wouldn't want Sam to think you didn't know how, would you?''

jimmy proves he's right

The long summer days passed quickly for Jimmy Fox. The heat of July gave way to the dry desert winds of August. Up before sunrise, Jimmy's first chore of the day was to hunt food for Sam. The little falcon had grown very fast. He had all his feathers now.

One morning Jimmy watched Sam in the large cage Jimmy had built for him. The bird opened his sharp beak wide. "Got a surprise for you today, Sam," Jimmy said. "Look!" He opened the paper sack he was carrying and took out a chunk of raw meat. He tossed the meat inside the cage. Sam caught it and swallowed it whole.

"It's time I taught you to fly, Sam," Jimmy told him. "You'll be surprised at the things *I've* learned in the last two months!"

He slipped the empty paper sack over Sam's head so that the bird would not be frightened. Then he took him out of the cage. With care he carried Sam outdoors, to the big joshua tree where he'd found him. "I'm setting you free, Sam," Jimmy said softly. "You're too big to live in a cage now."

When he removed the paper sack, Sam blinked against the bright sunlight. He stretched out his wings. Then he leaped upward. He flapped his wings, then circled higher and higher into the morning sunshine. At last he spread his wings to their fullest and glided down to land on the very top of the joshua.

"Well, I guess you can fly all right," Jimmy said. "Maybe someday you and I can go flying together!"

Jimmy walked back to the hangar alone. Would he ever see Sam again? He'd miss him, but it was Sam's right to be free. Jimmy knew what that meant, now that he'd learned to pilot the *Flying Falcon*. His fourteenth birthday was less than three weeks away now. When it came, he could fly solo — that is, if his father felt he was ready. He'd *really* be free then!

When Jimmy got back to the hangar he saw a strange car parked in front. Wondering who the caller could be, he walked toward the flight office in a corner of the building. He could hear low voices. His father was talking with someone. Then Jimmy knew the other voice — Wilson Gorman's!

He tried to tiptoe past the office door, but his father heard him. He called, "Come in here, Jimmy! We want to talk to you."

As Jimmy entered the office his father

said, "Son, Mr. Gorman made a special trip over here to thank you for saving his life when his plane crashed."

"Guess I owe you quite a lot, Jimmy." Gorman was smiling up at him. The man wore his leg in a cast. A pair of crutches leaned against the office wall.

Jimmy swallowed hard. "I only did what anybody would have done," he muttered.

"No, Jimmy! You risked your life — and I thank you. But now —" Gorman waited, then leaned forward. "I'd like to ask a favor of you. You see, when I got to the hospital I couldn't find my wallet. It must have dropped out of my pocket where the plane crashed. You didn't see it, did you, Jimmy?"

Jimmy was angry. "Of course not, Mr. Gorman," he answered hotly. "If I had, I'd have given it to you right away!"

Gorman coughed. Frank Fox looked away. There was a brief silence. Then

Gorman spoke. "Jimmy, I'd like to drive over to the crash site with you and have a look around."

Jimmy was silent as the two of them drove across the desert in Gorman's car. It was a four-wheel-drive rover. Gorman pulled up near the rocky field where his racer had crashed. The blackened remains were still there. Gorman got out. He set his crutches under his arms and made his way to the wreck. "Look around good, Jimmy," he said. "There was a lot of money in my wallet. I'll pay a real reward if you find it."

"You don't have to do that, sir," Jimmy said.

Gorman watched him closely as Jimmy looked under the wreck. Maybe Gorman thought he'd found the wallet and hidden it.

"There's nothing here," Jimmy said finally. "Look for yourself."

Gorman went back to the car and

climbed in. He mopped his forehead. Then he turned to Jimmy. "I'm taking you at your word, Jimmy." His voice was hard and flat. "But let me warn you. If I find out different, it'll go bad for you."

Without another word, he started up the car. "Get in!" he said sharply.

"I'd rather walk back," Jimmy said, turning away.

He watched Gorman's car drive off. Then he sat down on a rock. He thought, *This is the last time I'll ever help anybody!* Tears ran down his cheeks. He did not bother to wipe them away.

A soft noise whispered above him. He turned his wet face upward. There was Sam, gliding down to land on top of the joshua tree.

"Hi, Sam," Jimmy cried, jumping up. "Come on down. You're the only friend I've got!"

Sam cocked his head. He looked at

Jimmy for a long moment. Then he spread his great wings and flew off. Jimmy watched him fly high into the sky. An idea suddenly struck him. "Sam!" he cried." Did you—?"

He went to the joshua and looked up at the empty nest twenty feet above his head. Thorny leaves made it look impossible to climb. How could he reach the nest to look inside? He ran back to the house and got a pair of leather gloves. He put on long pants. Then he ran back to the joshua tree. Carefully he made his way up, inch by inch.

A thorn jabbed him in the leg. He paid no attention. Sharp thorns scratched his arms. He wiped at the blood and went on. Finally he reached the top. He looked inside the old nest of sticks and leaves. Something lay in the bottom! He couldn't quite see what it was.

With care he slid an arm into the big nest, feeling around with his fingers. He felt something — the wallet! He lifted it and stuck it inside his shirt. Then he slowly climbed down the tree.

Jimmy stood on the ground, thinking what to do next. Wilson Gorman wouldn't believe where he had found the wallet, would he? "I'll go tell Dad," he said to himself. "He'll know what to do."

Frank Fox was still in his office. Jimmy stood before his father's desk. Silently he took the wallet from his shirt and laid it on the desk. His father picked it up, turning it over and over. Then he looked at Jimmy's torn clothes and frowned.

He flipped the wallet open. There was a pilot's license inside. It read, "*Wilson Gorman, Commercial Pilot.*" He looked steadily into Jimmy's eyes. "All right, son. Tell me the truth."

Jimmy told his father just what had happened. How Gorman had suspected him, and had become angry. How Sam had made him look at the nest. How he'd climbed up and found the wallet inside.

Frank Fox came around the desk. He put his arm around Jimmy. "I believe you, son," he said. "But it'll be hard to make Wilson Gorman swallow your story!"

"I don't care *what* he thinks!" Jimmy exclaimed.

"Leave Mr. Gorman to me, Jimmy. I'll handle this my way."

Jimmy turned to leave, but his father stopped him. "Be careful how you judge people, Jimmy," he said slowly. "Everybody has two sides—good and bad. You just happened to see the man's bad side. Now, let's fly the Super Cub over to Gorman's field and return his wallet."

Wilson Gorman met the Super Cub at the parking ramp. "What brings you here, Frank?" he asked.

"Tell him, Jimmy," Frank Fox said.

"I found your wallet, Mr. Gorman. Here."

Gorman took the wallet from Jimmy's outstretched hand. He opened it. He counted the money inside, the way Jimmy knew he would.

"I think you'll find nothing missing, Wilson," Jimmy's father said.

"No, it's all here. Now tell me, Jimmy," Gorman said, his voice thick as syrup. "Just where did you find it? We looked all over. Remember?"

"It was up on top of a big joshua tree," Jimmy blurted out. Then he was sorry he had said that. It sounded like a big fib.

"You'll need no explanation from my son, Wilson," his father cut in. "You have your wallet back. I'll thank you not to hurt Jimmy's feelings." Without another word, father and son taxied out to the runway and took off.

That night at dinner, Frank Fox told

Jimmy's mother what had happened. Debbie Fox threw her head back and laughed. "What a silly thing," she said. "I can hardly blame Wilson for being that way. Imagine finding his wallet in a treetop!"

"Well, we'd best forget about it now," Frank Fox said. "It's getting close to bedtime. Tomorrow we'll do some slope soaring, over by West Mountain."

"Gee, Dad!" Jimmy exclaimed. "We've never done that!"

"I know, son. You'll learn there's lots of different ways to fly a sailplane. Maybe you'll never get as good as Sam. But I'll bet you'll find that bird over there tomorrow."

"Why, Dad?" Jimmy asked.

"The radio said there's a cold front coming. That's when the slope winds are best."

He explained to Jimmy how cold air

blows down off the North Pacific Ocean, and how it moves across the Mojave Desert, pushing underneath the warm air next to the sand.

"When that happens, Jimmy, the cold air forces the warm air up. And where the cold and warm air meet is called a front," Frank Fox explained.

"Then can you soar along the front, riding on the rising air currents?" Jimmy asked.

"That's right, Jimmy," his father said. "But frontal soaring is not for beginners. It can be very dangerous. When the warm air is pushed up, the water vapor in it cools and makes clouds. A whole line of thunderstorms can start. They have extra-strong updrafts. So strong they can tear the wings right off a sailplane."

Frank Fox paused to let Jimmy think about what he had just said. Then he went on. "Thunderstorms can make big

hail stones. They can break your windshield. Whenever you see a thunderstorm forming, stay well clear of it!''

''What about slope soaring, Dad?'' Jimmy asked.

''Well, that's different. When the wind

blows over a mountain range, it acts like a big wave in the sky. Sailplane pilots can ride on mountain waves, just like surfers ride ocean waves coming up on a beach.''

Jimmy was excited. He could hardly wait for tomorrow! He listened carefully. His father told him how other waves in the sky form behind the first wave. Just like waves behind a big rock in a swift river.

''That's how soaring pilots can fly across country,'' his father went on. ''They soar up high on one wave, glide down to the next, then climb up again, over and over.''

Other sailplane pilots, Jimmy learned, fly across country another way. They do it by climbing up inside a rising thermal bubble. Then they slide down the sky to reach the next thermal, and so on.

''Thermal bubbles form when the sun heats up the sand on the desert floor,'' his father said. "At times, the air rises so fast it makes little whirlpools. You've seen them, Jimmy. They're called dust devils."

Jimmy nodded. He remembered how a dust devil had whirled around him one day when he was out hiking. It looked like a small tornado. Sand and dry sticks were sucked up, sweeping around and around, until the dust devil passed by.

an exciting solo flight

Jimmy marked off the days on the wall calendar in his bedroom. There was so much to do. He had to get ready for his first solo flight on the day he'd turn fourteen. There was a whole pile of books to study. Books his father gave him. Books about the weather. Books about how to find your way across the land in an airplane, day or night, in good weather or bad.

Each day they flew the *Flying Falcon,* except when the cold fronts brought rain storms. Then Jimmy stayed inside the hangar, washing and polishing the sailplane. It was his and he loved it. Loved to look at it. And best, he loved to fly it.

Sam appeared now and then, gliding down on his wide wings to land near the hangar. Whenever he showed up, Jimmy went to the kitchen and brought him a scrap of meat.

Then came a long time when Sam did

not come at all. Jimmy was worried about what might have happened to him. Now, on each flight he took along a pair of binoculars. He searched the desert floor for the falcon, but Sam was nowhere to be seen.

Then one day when Jimmy and his father were soaring in a strong thermal, he spotted something down below. "Dad!" he cried. "There's Sam! He's caught in a trap!"

Frank Fox reached for the binoculars. "It's Sam, all right," he said. "Let's go take a closer look!"

They banked over steeply. Jimmy pulled the lever that opened the spoilers so that they could come down faster. At 500 feet above the desert floor they circled over a dry river. They could see Sam's foot caught in the jaws of a steel trap.

They turned the sailplane away, toward the airport, diving for speed. They landed, rolling to a stop beside the yellow airport jeep. They climbed into it and raced the jeep across the desert to rescue Sam.

When they found him, Sam seemed almost nothing but skin and bones and feathers. He could barely open his eyes when Jimmy sprung the trap and picked him up. "Come on, Sam," Jimmy said softly. "I'm taking you home."

The first week in September passed. As Jimmy's birthday drew near, he flew the *Flying Falcon* every chance he had. His father was always with him, in the rear seat, teaching him new things, correcting his mistakes.

Sam got better. Soon he was flying again on strong wings. Now he'd be gone for days at a time. Sometimes he would show up in the evening for a scrap of meat. He would gulp it down, then fly off again.

Finally came September the fourteenth,

the day before Jimmy's fourteenth birthday.

"Tomorrow's the big day, Jimmy," his father said at the dinner table. "Think you're ready to solo?"

Jimmy grinned. "I am if you say so, Dad!"

"Well, son, you've been flying well these past weeks. How much flying time have you in your logbook?"

"I've got twelve hours and fifteen minutes flying with you, Dad!" Jimmy replied quickly.

"Then, if the weather holds tomorrow, and you give me a good ride, we'll see what happens."

"Swell!" Jimmy said. "And — can I take Sam along with me? I promised him I would!"

Frank Fox laughed. "You're not supposed to carry passengers, Jimmy, until you get your Private License, but I guess Sam's special. All you need to fly solo is a Student Pilot license. You'll get that tomorrow in town, from the government flight examiner. Then, when I sign your logbook, it means I think you're safe and ready to fly alone."

"Happy birthday, Jimmy!" The government flight examiner shook Jimmy's hand. Jimmy studied his Student Pilot license. He could hardly believe what was happening.

"Thank you, sir!" he managed.

Driving back to Morning Sun Airfield, Jimmy's father told him what they were going to do next. "Bud will tow us up over West Mountain, Jimmy," he said. "You and I will cut loose and soar around awhile. Then, I want you to bring me back to the airport. Make a good landing, between the white lines. I'll not say a word. You'll be on your own."

The air was glassy smooth, the afternoon sun low. Jimmy's father said, "Now."

Jimmy pulled the tow release. He swept the *Flying Falcon* around in a climbing turn to the right. He was heading for West Mountain. The wind was from the west. Soon he found a strong updraft in the slope wind.

The updraft carried them almost to 3,000 feet. They swept back and forth, along the ridge, always turning away from the mountain into the west wind, for safety.

"Okay, Jimmy," his father called from behind him. "That's fine. Let's go home now."

Jimmy swung the *Flying Falcon* around and headed for Morning Sun Airfield, ten miles away. The wind and the sun were behind them. The tail wind made the sailplane fly faster across the desert floor. They arrived over the field in under ten minutes.

Jimmy studied the airport, deciding which way to land. They were nearly a thousand feet above the field. He made a gliding turn, into the traffic pattern, along the north side of the field. Then he turned downwind.

When things looked right to him, Jimmy swung the *Flying Falcon* across the wind. They were at 500 feet now, coming down.

The wind was stronger the closer they got to the ground. A wind shear, his father would call it. For a tense moment Jimmy feared he'd waited too long to turn onto the final approach to land. But his long practice came to his aid. Confidently, he turned toward the runway early, reaching it with room to spare.

The sailplane picked up speed as they crossed the end of the runway. He flew low, only inches above the runway, in what his father called ground effect.

They floated along. Jimmy knew he could land right beside his mother and sister, standing beside the runway at midfield and waving.

Jimmy pulled the spoilers lever and set the *Flying Falcon* down, right between the white lines. He eased the stick forward. The sailplane skidded to a smooth stop in the soft sand.

"That's fine, Jimmy!" Frank Fox said,

climbing out of the cockpit. "Here, hand me your logbook." He took it from Jimmy and wrote, *James Fox, age 14, is ready for solo flight*.

Jimmy Fox felt very much alone. The rear seat was empty, like a huge cave. There was only the noise of the wind outside. He rode at the end of the tow rope, climbing higher and higher into the late afternoon sky.

His father was flying the tow plane, toward West Mountain. Only Sam was with him in the sailplane. The falcon perched on the seat back near Jimmy's head.

"Okay, Sam," Jimmy told him. "Now I'll show you how I can fly!"

He glanced at the altimeter. They were 1500 feet high. Time for release! He reached for the handle and pulled. The tow rope snapped forward. Jimmy swung around in a climbing turn to the right. He was flying! *Flying solo*. Free at last!

He settled down to business. The sailplane was lighter now without his father in the back seat. The controls felt different. He handled them smoothly and well. As if he'd flown solo all his life.

The low sun made dark shadows across the desert floor. There were dark shadows of drifting clouds above him. Jimmy studied the shadows, watching to see how fast they moved.

"Wind's right out of the west, Sam," he said. "Of course *you* know that! I'd say it's blowing about twenty knots."

He banked the slender wings over and turned toward the slope of West Mountain. He held a steady course until he felt the *Flying Falcon* begin to rise. He soared along the ridge until all lift was gone. Then he turned for home.

"Let's fly around a little on the way back, Sam," he said. He flew in great S-turns, enjoying the beauty of the desert below. The sailplane drifted farther and farther away from Morning Sun Airfield. Then Jimmy glanced at the altimeter. It didn't look right. He gasped. They were down to only 500 feet!

"Sam!" he cried. "We can't make the field!"

In the shadows, the sailplane sank lower and lower toward the rocky floor. There were no thermals to be found.

"Sam! I'm afraid we're going to crash!" Jimmy cried. "What'll I do?"

As if in reply, Sam began to peck at the plane's canopy. "Okay, I'll let you out, Sam," Jimmy said. "No use both of us crash landing!"

He opened the canopy latch. Sam dove out, into the slipstream, unfolding his long wings. Jimmy watched him go. He was really alone now. He wondered, does Sam think I'm a terrible pilot?

Then he saw a flash of light. It was Sam, circling higher and higher in the sunlight. "You've found a thermal!"

Jimmy yelled. "Wait for me, Sam!"

Soon they were flying beside each other, in easy circles, higher and higher. "Thanks, Sam!" Jimmy called out. "You sure saved my day!"

Jimmy was extra-careful to stay well

inside the thermal bubble, until the altimeter read 4,000 feet. Sam was flying beside him. Jimmy could see Morning Sun Airfield now. A little higher and he'd feel safe leaving the thermal to glide home.

Then everything turned a milky white. The desert floor was gone. He'd flown right inside a big cloud. Something his father had warned him against *ever* doing!

"Sam!" Jimmy cried out. "Where are you? What'll I do now?"

The sailplane shook and bounced, like the jeep bouncing over a rough trail. A wing pointed down. Jimmy fought to keep it level. He could barely hold onto the control stick.

He tried hard to keep looking at the instruments. He tried to remember what his father had told him to do. *When there is nothing outside to see, use your instruments.*

"Needle ... ball ... airspeed ..." he repeated from memory. "Keep the turn needle centered. Keep the ball centered. And be sure to keep the airspeed up."

It rushed back to him, all that his father had taught him. When the sailplane banks, watch the turn needle. The steeper the bank, the faster the turn and the farther out the needle moves.

"Keep the ball centered with the rudders," he said to himself. "If the ball moves out to the left, I kick it back with my left foot!"

A big bump shook the controls from his hand. Jimmy shoved forward on the stick. "Watch the airspeed most of all!" he said aloud. "If it slows down, I'll stall and the plane won't fly! If it's too fast, pull the stick back, gently!"

Jimmy forced everything else from his mind now. He even forgot Sam. All he could think of was keeping the sailplane under control while inside the cloud.

The wind grew worse. He was being carried upward faster now. The altimeter needle swung around and around ... 5,000 feet ... 6,000 feet ... 7,000 feet!

There came a loud hammering. Hail stones hit the canopy. Jimmy ducked. Then the darkness inside the cloud grew lighter. Above him all was a milky white. Then the *Flying Falcon* shot out of the cloud — into clear sky!

Jimmy gasped. Huge clouds piled up all around him. He was trapped inside a cloud canyon! But it was so beautiful, so exciting, that he wasn't so afraid. The knot in his stomach went away.

The towering clouds were a bright white, like great castles in the air. He glanced at the compass. He was heading west.

In awe, Jimmy studied the giant cloud directly ahead of the sailplane. It towered thousands of feet high. It bent over into

an ugly shape, its top flattened by strong winds.

Jimmy took stock. He knew that as long as he stayed clear of the clouds he could see where he was going. He tried circling for lift, back toward the east, inside the cloud canyon. In the distance he saw the clouds form steep canyon walls. He headed for the V they formed.

It was cold in the high sky. Only the tops of the clouds were still in sunlight. In the cloud canyon it was growing dark. Then he couldn't even see the canyon. He'd flown right into the canyon wall!

The *Flying Falcon* came out of the other side of the cloud. Up ahead Jimmy saw Sam.

"Wait for me!" he yelled.

He pushed the sailplane's nose down a little, to pick up extra speed. He was flying at more than a hundred miles an hour. The wind made a loud noise. He could see the V growing larger as he flew toward it, but he was sinking too fast. Could he make it?

Then he saw Sam soaring upward. He followed Sam and felt the rustle of lift on the wings. He held his breath. It was barely enough to squeeze into the V.

"Thanks, Sam!" Jimmy sighed. "We made it out of the storm!"

The desert floor was almost pitch black now. Jimmy had drifted far from Morning Sun Airfield while flying inside the storm cloud. He'd never make it home!

He felt sick inside. He circled down, down, down, into the dark night. Then, in the distance, he saw a flashing green and white beacon. Wilson Gorman's airport! He had no other choice. He turned the *Flying Falcon* and headed for the beacon.

The sailplane touched down gently at midfield. Jimmy steered it off the runway right onto the parking ramp. He opened the canopy and got out. His legs felt rubbery.

Wilson Gorman came out of his flight office, walking without crutches. "What brings you here, Jimmy?" he asked in surprise.

"I got trapped inside a storm cloud," Jimmy admitted. "I'm sorry, Mr. Gorman. There was no place else to land!"

Gorman laughed. "I guess I owe you an apology, Jimmy," he said. "So, maybe it was more than luck that brought you here."

Jimmy followed Wilson Gorman into the flight office. He borrowed the telephone and called Morning Sun Airfield.

"I'm okay, Dad," he said when Frank Fox answered.

"Where are you, son?" his father asked, his voice tight with worry.

"Over at Mr. Gorman's. Will you come and get me, Dad?"

"Just tie down the *Flying Falcon,* Jimmy. I'll drive over right away. We'll bring the plane home tomorrow."

Jimmy hung up. He was suddenly tired — but happy. He'd flown solo, gotten into bad trouble, and then gotten out of it — by himself. That is, with Sam's help. He began to laugh.

"What's so funny, Jimmy?" Gorman asked, handing him a cup of hot chocolate.

"It's Sam," Jimmy answered. "Sam found your wallet for you. Now he's saved my life. And *I* was going to teach *him* how to fly! He's the greatest bird in the whole world!"

"That's what's so wonderful about flying, Jimmy," Gorman said. "You never know what will happen next!"

Jimmy sipped the chocolate and smiled to himself. Mr. Gorman wasn't such a bad guy, after all!

Full of adventure and suspense, *Jimmy Fox And The Flying Falcon* is the exciting story of a boy who, more than anything else in the world, wanted to fly airplanes. Jimmy was the youngest member of a famous aviation family known as the Flying Foxes. He had grown up at the California desert airfield owned by his father, a veteran airman. Flying was in his blood. But Jimmy was only fourteen, which meant that he had to wait two whole years before he could even try for his Student Pilot license. The waiting was almost more than he could bear. But everything changed the day Jimmy's father surprised him with the gift of the beautiful white sailplane. How Jimmy learned to fly it—and what happened then—add up to an action-packed story that will hold even a "reluctant" reader from first page to last. The text has been carefully expertised by authorities for easy vocabulary.

Don Dwiggins writes about flying from years of first-hand experience. A seasoned airman, he has logged almost 10,000 flying hours as a first pilot. During World War II he was a flight instructor with Britain's Royal Air Force and also flew with the U.S. Air Force Glider Corps. He has written more than 30 popular books about aviation for both young people and adults, as well as thousands of magazine and newspaper articles on flying. He is presently Senior Editor for *Plane and Pilot* magazine.

Olga Dwiggins was born and grew up in Ontario, Canada. Her ambition was to become an artist so she came to the United States to study art, first at the Otis Art Institute and then at Art Center in Los Angeles. Subsequently she illustrated costume designs for motion pictures, then entered the fashion field, doing fashion illustrations for women and children. Mrs. Dwiggins is a flying enthusiast and often flies with her husband in his private plane. The Dwiggins' make their home in Malibu, California.